RED TULIP

A Novelette by

Rasheed Hafeez

ISBN: 978-1-7342540-1-3

R.D. Talley Books Publishing, LLC
P.O. Box 271029
Las Vegas, Nevada 89127
www.rdtalleybooks.com

PROLOGUE

A symphony of noise like the move of an electric current through a conduit rent the air in a thoroughly-lit stadium for the Women National Basketball Association competition between two women's teams.

As the supporters for each team joggled songs between them, one hardly heard the commentators' performances as their voice seemed to have been swallowed-up by the myriad of voices from the stand. The direction of the ball on the court did not fail to determine the movement of the loudest plaudits just as a conductor determines the flow of an orchestra.

My team in burgundy, gold and black rode through mountains and valleys before making it to this grand stage this year, having seen our last two attempts fallen through.

We went up against a team whose physique could best be matched by outstanding display of creativity, without which will render their rivals almost useless. The other team, putting on a blue, purple and yellow jersey was also on fire as we both hustled to make a point for our teams.

Instructions flew out of the nest of each team's coach as they hoped to get some accolades for a job well done. And at every junction when things didn't go as planned, you'd see a bit of frustration written boldly on the chalkboard of their faces.

The air-conditioned stadium couldn't shove aside the sweltering sweat dripping from each player's body as they fought hard to get their team's name crested on a gold-plated trophy.

'Jameela, get us the trophy! Bring it home baby,' a broad male voice roared from among the spectators rang through my head but I couldn't ascertain where such a remark came from.

Right from the beginning of the competition, I stood out from the rest of my fellow teammates, being the star of the team. What gave me another distinct quality that caught the undiluted attention of many was my mode of dressing. I overheard some fans saying in the cafeteria one day.

'She's got some aura of decency and integrity,' one of them remarked.

The other person replied, 'No wonder she's on top of her game always.'

I walked, showing no sign of eavesdropping on their remarks. I wore my favourite hijab which my dearest husband bought for me during the christening of my last child and a black body stretch suit underneath my uniform to swathe my bare body.

And as one of the opposing team players broke forth with the ball, I tactically stole the ball from her to the astonishing surprise of all the seated spectators and pushed the ball with a dexterous energy down to the other end of the court. I swiftly, without giving it second thought, went for a three-point shot, which I made hitch-free.

And within me, I could sense the synergy of exhilaration between my bones and marrow that I've really made myself, family, and country proud. Throughout the entire season, I became the Most Valuable Player which was more of a healing balm for me.

Seated amongst the spectators was the love of my life, whose immeasurable support had led me through the thorns and thistles of being a woman of the cloth in a sport that barely focused on being a strength for the Muslimahs. He settled-in on time with my worlds whom Allah had gifted me to cheer me to victory.

Following my successful three-pointer shot, I looked towards their direction and my six-year-old Nadeera screamed with her lovely tiny voice, 'That's right Ummi!' I beamed with a smile and waved back at her.

Back into the game as it got to its climax, I became the centre of attraction in no time and I kept on firing my side to the unbelievable victory with some of my runs, which I had wore as a garb during training, and some incredible passes to my co-player, revealing how cohesive we are with teamwork. An attempt by a fellow colleague to send the ball to the other end was defensively blocked, though came back to me straight. Your guess was a good as mine with what I did with the ball. I sent the whole stadium ablaze after shooting the ball to register another stupendous three-pointer.

The happy look written boldly on my face said it all but….I felt a part of my body was unbolted as I clenched my chest, following a sudden pain that traveled at the speed of light all over my body. My world seemed rushing to crash down right in my presence. I felt numb. My vision became blurry. Suddenly, all that I could hear were eerie voices.

Myriads of thoughts ran through my mind almost immediately. Everything around me got drowned as well. And straight to the ground did I collapse. In the midst of this, I felt a stop in the sound oozing out of the crowd's mouths like a stoppage time at the end of a 90-minute contest.

'Baby! Baby get up!' Bilal, with tears rolling down his cheeks, broke through the circle as he came rushing towards the spot where I was to be attended to by the medics and knelt beside me.

'Sir! Could you please step back?' One of the medics tried to lift Bilal up away from his wife, the fallen hero.

'No, this is my wife!' he responded with an eye-turned-red expression like a burning coal.

In a softer tone now, the doctor patting Bilal on the back said, 'I know you're concerned but you must allow us work.'

Everything was speedily becoming a heap of ashes right in front of me. My husband was insisting that he stayed beside me. I heard the coach tell my sweetheart emotionally, 'Mr. Raheem let the Doctors do their job!' That was the first time I saw the coach driven to tears.

And that also invited a teary smile which got my cheeks stained. Bilal cast a long-lost look at the coach got up and stepped back. The team doctor began to work on me and the first injection hibernated me as I shut my eyes from the world.

1

The whole atmosphere in the Queens Community Center at a late afternoon was thrown into turmoil as many feet gathered to witness the thrashing of The Ladies of Faith by the indomitable Mount Vernon Valkyries.

With the fourth quarter in sight, one couldn't imagine the manner of dejection that was boldly written on the faces of The Ladies of Faith players since they were losing to the Valkyries by the score of 86-73.

This manner of loss had never been recorded between these two female squads before. The cheers from the winning team's fans came like a roaring wind ready for a tsunami considering the one-minute left on the clock to witness the death of the match.

Though strength was stretched beyond its capabilities, The Ladies were nowhere near the power of Samson the Valkyries requested for prior to this encounter as the latter's players engaged their contenders as one on melodeum.

Wisdom was employed by the Valkyries as one of their players stole the ball from their opponents to bag a three-pointer which remarkably accrued massive plaudits from the undying spectators.

'You can't stop this, Catholic schoolgirl! Stick to praying, not B-ball,' a Caucasian Valkyrie player on jersey number one passed a mocking comment on the Ladies of Faith players.

Brittany Cedowski, the skipper of the Ladies of Faith team, buried her head in shame having looked at the clock which showed they barely had thirty seconds to redeem their damnable image. The best she could do was to gnash her teeth as she walked away.

From the side of the court, there stood a woman who had her hair covered just like one of the nuns coming out from Coventry. Sister Clarence wore 'The Ladies of Faith' jumpsuit. Shouts of instruction flew out of her mouth in desperation with a view to getting her team to scoop out points from the duel. Sister Clarence broke her vocal cords, yelling at her players to get to the other end of the court.

In no time, Brittany took possession of the ball and forced it down the court to the amazement of the onlookers. She let the ball slip off her hands to the waiting hands of one of her teammates, Jenny Shales, on jersey number three.

Jenny let the ball travel to jersey number two, Henrietta Wilkerson, who later passed the ball to Nancy Wells on jersey number 5, following her show of brilliance from the end of the court while the clock ticked away.

Every one of Nancy's moves to get past the Valkyrie's defense was all to no avail as the opponent's player already anticipated her moves wholly. Suddenly the jersey number four, Joana Hansberg, with a plaited cocktail braided hair, moved into position and signaled Nancy to send the ball to her.

'Nancy!', Joana called out to her teammate in a husky voice though carrying a look that showed a loss. At the very instance when Joana received the ball, she drove it straight to the basket with an attempt to dunk it. However, as she took a shot, it was blocked and stolen by the other team to her disappointment.

Another Valkyrie team member took advantage of that as she pushed the ball forcefully down the court. Though the Ladies of Faith tried all they could to keep up, they were helpless as they watched her dunk the ball right in the basket. And the sound of the buzzer travelled through the air as it sent the stadium into a frenzy zone.

Tears strolled down the sweaty-eyes of Brittany who stumped over with her hands on her knees after looking at the scoreboard to see the final score, 92-73. She buried her head in the sepulchre of utmost disappointment. Sister Clarence's call lifted her head from among the shameful dead where she buried it.

'It's okay ladies. Wheel it in. You all did a good job.' Sister Clarence did the sign of crucifixion as the ladies gathered. She quickly led them in reciting the Hail Mary Creed.

That loss saw St. Mary's Catholic High School lose the game in an unpremeditated way. Supporters who had travelled to witness the encounter exited the venue in silence. While some grumbled about poor officiating, others did not but showed their hatred for some of the players who performed below par performance.

'What in God's name can you call that?', an angry fan blasted out his thought as he kicked a can lying fallow right in front of him.

'The officials were poor in their judgment and couldn't have watched that slip away from our team,' another fan spoke out with sheer annoyance.

'Do you call that teamwork from those who lacked faith in themselves from the outset?' The first fan questioned the lack of teamwork among the players.

The Ladies of Faith players couldn't muster the courage to come out and confront their challenger. Everywhere was as silent as the graveyard. The players' breathing became the only means of communication. Sister Clarence tried to gear them up. Nothing upset them other than the fact that the unbelievers defeated them in a landslide victory. Shouts could be heard from the stadium.

Despite the almost one-hour ago victory, the Valkyrie players rode triumphantly around the court as they sing mockingly the 'Alleluia' song. That song saw the Ladies of Faith players plunge themselves into a more sorrowful state.

That melancholic state stayed with them for as long as they stayed. They grudgingly got on the bus to convey them back home. What was left of them was nothing but the debris of shame from their disappointing outing.

'We lost when we could have won the game,' Brittany spoke out her mind with bitterness written all over her face. 'This shouldn't be the end as we failed today to rise another day.'

2

Prayer in our house usually began our early morning routine and capped it all when the dusk prepared to go to bed. Before the dawn washed off its face with the morning mist, it was expected of us all in the house to have had our bath since my dad usually led my brothers and me in Fajr prayer.

This morning wasn't in anyway different at all as I had woken up even before my alarm went all the way to vomit its eerie sound from its belly. I should have cast away the alarm bell fixed to my bedside by my father since but couldn't because it represented a huge signal that I had woken up.

As I prepared to go for the early Morning Prayer, I took a last glance at my mother's picture, which she had taken in her jersey. She was dressed in baggy hoodies and gym shoes, and her hijabs were styled into a bun. While I peered into the picture the more, I tried all I could to figure out how she would have looked now that I'm a grown up. Should I say I missed her affectionate cuddling as a mother or not?

Before I could finish looking at the picture of the most loving woman in my life, I heard a call with a shrill voice from my dad as if the adhan was being called by Prophet Muhammad's (SAW) acolyte, Bilal, which coincidentally is my dad's name, just that he was not as dark as the dark horse who followed the teachings of the Prophet's (PBUH).

Anytime my dad sat us down to narrate how Bilal joined the Prophet's (PBUH) train.

My dad kept an unusual garden in which none except him and my mother tendered when she was alive. I stepped into my mother's shoes after her demise and that became my every morning routine before the Fajr prayer, meaning I had to wake up before anybody could think of regaining their consciousness from the previous night's hibernation.

As I walked around the garden watering the flowers, I saw my favourite which was also my mom's. All that was left for me to remember was that she always fastened each flower like a brooch on my cloth whenever I set out for school.

The Tulip this morning appeared withered. That got me worried as I tried to pick the puzzles together as to the perpetrator of that. At the very instant, I knew my mom would not only wear a worrying look on her face but would have also found out who did that and for what reason.

I straightened the petals and re-inserted the stalk into the earth. After stepping away from the white Tulips, I saw my favourite- Red Tulip. I never missed plucking it in a day to fasten it on my cloth as it had been bringing good luck to me since my childhood, which I was told later by my mother. My love for Tulip was undiluted and non-negotiable.

Having been carried away by the extra care I gave to my flower, it took me some time before I could hear my dad, who sent his voice to miles to get my attention after peeping to check me out in the garden.

'Hey, Baba wassup?! You almost scared the life outta me!' I had to quickly release the hand gloves around my wrist, wash my hands as usual and set out to meet him.

'Come on in! Your brothers have already eaten and left. You could have caught a ride were you faster than you thought.' My father spoke softly through a wry smile flowing from his lips.

Anytime my father seemed to be displeased with an action of mine, he seldom handled it the way a child would handle the pain from underneath the bosom. At this point in time, I did nothing more than grab my book bag and basketball.

As I set out for school, I swiftly cast a last look on my room, switched off the light, and turned on the alarm should there be any break in. For six years and a half now, we've not had another case of the burglaries in the neighbourhood after Mr. Simpson's. We weren't too familiar with the Simpsons because on the one hand, he's a Christian and on the other hand an alcoholic. And my father passionately loathed every form of drinking spree which he referred to as Haram. Nonetheless, the tragedy that befell Mr. Dave Simpson struck everybody including the children in the neighbourhood. No day will go by without seeing feet trooping to commiserate with him.

From what we later heard, the burglar was one of the security personnel assigned to our boulevard, because without that, it wouldn't have been so easy for the perpetrator to go unscathed when each building has its own alarm bell that would ordinarily have gone haywire should there be any interference.

With time scurrying away like the winged-chariots of fire, I rushed into the kitchen to meet my father taking care of the dirty dishes. Since the demise of my mother, my dad never allowed us to go into the kitchen except on rare occasions when he would be too busy attending to visitors.

Thus, we've gotten used to that act of his, especially when we get ready to leave for school. I took my sit behind the table already set with different kinds of fruit and the delicacy for the day. And I began to dish out the breakfast meal, which my mother used to do when she was alive, from the dishes on the table. I scooped into my plate what I could eat at a go because wastefulness, according to my dad, is a taboo in Islam.

'Assalam Alaikum Warahmatullahi Wabarakatuh,' I greeted him with my head crouched.

'Wa'Alaikum Salam Warahmatullahi Wabarakatuh. What were you doing up there? Breakfast has been ready for almost twenty minutes,' he answered without taking his eyes off the plates he was washing.

In my mind, his undaunted care flashed through and I began meditating on his manner of love. Since I knew my right from left, he never for once showed any sign of being tired though wrinkles have started growing in some edges on his body.

Whenever I walked up to him in the garden while looking after the flowers like the first bath a new child would get after birth, I found in his face the passion I stole years later. He would especially give all his care for the Tulips. And that drew my attention to the flower.

While this thought was still running in my mind, he interrupted my flow. He interrupted having turned around for the first time to notice how I was dressed. His look told me immediately that he wasn't too pleased with that.

'Why do you always wear such clothes to school?' He asked with disgust written all over his face as he was trying to arrange the washed plates.

'Baba, you know I'm meeting with Khadijah after school.' I replied in a manner that would remind him of my mother. Each time I stepped on his toes which should have incurred his wrath upon me, talking in this manner which I have spoken, to her, always hit his soft spot and that a smile will be formed around his bearded mouth.

My dad knew I was telling the truth about my meeting after school with the only friend he allowed to keep my company. This he did having gotten wind of the kind of family Khadijah came from. He never for once took his mind off the path of giving my entirety for my school studies even though he also expected me to devote more of my time for the Qu'ran.

'Dad! I get straight A's and I go to halaqa classes on Thursdays and Sundays,' reminding him of what he already knew is as good as fueling a fired-up building. His grin look would make you have no other option than to smile or walk away.

'Yeah, but you still need to get in the Qu'ran. You're a young lady and soon to be an adult. It's time to concentrate on what is more important first,' he ended that with a tone of finality. I was not expected to continue the discussion from where he stopped it.

My application to colleges in earnest was also paramount to him as he worked all day to ensure no stone is left unturned. Despite the fact that I still have a whopping two more years to study in the high school, he had started asking questions if I had submitted some applications to colleges and went further to admonish me to start taking college tours. One of his strongest beliefs was that the early bird catches the worm. And after accepting the fact that I'd start the application as soon as possible, he went back to my mode of dressing.

'You can start dressing more like a lady. I bought you three Abayas for your birthday and you have not worn them yet.' I gnashed my teeth as I cast a thorough look at myself for the last time, and my response took him off his seat as he grabbed his keys to leave.

While he was heading towards the exit, he offered his usual last piece of advice before shutting the door behind him. I could see his grey hair had added strength from his hind-head. I smiled to myself shyly as I allowed his manner of treating me like the apple of his eyes flood my heart. I continued with my food knowing well that I had a train to board so as not to be late to school.

Despite the fact that my feet took me hurriedly to the train station, I could only get on board Number 7 train which was the last train heading towards my direction. The train had about seventeen coaches. After I got on board, I sat with my basketball firmly knitted to my hand. This morning was quite unusual as oceans of people from all walks of life were on board as well en route to their different destination.

'Never had it been like this before,' I said facing one of the passengers before.

'Are you new in this neighbourhood?' His question made me feel embarrassed and I, without being told, turned and rested my head on the window pane. I shut my eyes to escape from this world.

Before I knew it, we'd arrived at my school having been brought back to life by the resounding trumpeting of the train. I dragged my bag along with me and walked with other students who swiftly made their ways to school before the morning bell went off.

There was a different decoration at the school entrance with the inscription 'Welcome Back to School.' What was written wasn't as important as how it was written. I quickly headed down the corridor jam-packed with a lot of students by now who were trying to find their way to their classes. I almost ran into Caleb, the Most Handsome Sophomore.

'Hey, girl, watch out!' Caleb screamed out as he skated past me.

"Watch your tongue dude!" I replied without a second thought. Few of the bystanders who overheard my response, including myself, couldn't believe their eyes that that really came from me. I broke the silence with a rapid turn towards my locker to arrange my books inside and position my basketball rightly.

Just as I was about to close it, Khadijah showed up from nowhere. I had never seen her clad in the type of Hijab she wore. It was a pinkish-embroidered material, which she neatly packed with a silver brooch. Before we became friends, I was envious of her dress sense as she was the talk of the school. Everybody, without exempting me, thought she was proud.

I would never have forgotten how our paths crossed. We were supposed to go for a basketball competition. After school, I would always wait for a few practices. I was practicing one day when she walked up to me to ask if she could pair up with me for the workout. Since then, both of us have become the song the whole school sings.

'Assalam Alaikum,' she said as she opens her arms to embrace me.

'Wa Alaikum Salaam,' my response came with a childish laughter. We exchanged glances and unleashed a raucous laughter that caught everybody's attention in the corridor. As we were heading towards the English class that would start in earnest, we talked about the summer that's forthcoming and that changed my mood.

'You see, my sister in Islam, I have summer full of summer halaqa classes and college prep classes,' I said as of one in a drunken state. She laughed it off.

'Anyways, what are you doing after school?' she asked stylishly. Anytime Khadijah wanted us to go somewhere or do something together, she would pretend as if she was not even interested in that thing from the outset. I knew where she was coming from and gave her a quick response.

'Probably some ball, why?'

'Long Island just upgraded their basketball court. Let's go check it out,' she said apologetically. The Island she wanted us to go was two hours away by MTA New York bus as well as the train system. And my promise to my dad was to be home by 5:00 pm which mustn't fail. She quickly offered to drive us there herself in her father's black Lexus E360 Series since it would be after school. I acquiesced to the offer though had to remind her that my getting home by 5:00 pm was non-negotiable.

During the math class, my undivided attention was given to Mr. Carlos, whose Spanish accent was quite enticing that we desired to be in his class. My sitting mate was missing again for the third time this week and we had already got used to his absence, perhaps because his father was a member of the trustee of the school.

At 3:00 pm, we left the school as we faced the route that leads to the Long Island Catholic Community Center. Before we knew it, we had arrived at the gym. And as we walked into the ultra-modern spacious gym, our mouths were left open. My basketball was by my side as it was firmly tucked between my arm and hips.

'Dang! This court is nice. I see why it costs $5 to get in.' I couldn't keep my exasperation within me for that long. Khadijah came over to steal the ball away from me unannounced. She ran the court and did a lay-up. I went after her like a ravaging storm, hustled the ball from her and took a three-point shot outside the penalty spot.

We went on playing around on the court against each other. Hardly had we settled in before the Ladies of Faith team walked into the gym. I never knew that all along the team members have been acknowledging our versatility on the neatly-scrubbed court. However, some few comments caught our attention and caused us to stop abruptly after I took a shot which bounced in the direction of the team's captain, who grabbed the ball.

'You lose something?' Brittany asked with disgust written all over her face as she tossed the ball back to me. She told us they have been having scheduled practice there every day at about the same time.

'Okay, so you need this side of the court!' I said with a sheepish smile coming from my lips.

'No! We practise using the whole court,' Nancy, another girl on the team replied me with a snobbish attitude. I felt disgusted at her reply and I spilt out our ignorance that they would be using the same court.

'It's not your fault but could you please move along so we can get going with our practice?', the team's skipper asked with her face turned down as she was trying to lace up her boots.

'How do we know that? You're just telling us!' I reverted with indignation boldly flying out of my mouth.

'We don't need to lie to someone the likes of you. Just get off the court!' A girl from the team who now stood beside Brittany puffed up her attitude.

'And what is that supposed to mean?' I gave her my own bite back without thinking twice. When it almost turned to squabbles between the lady and me, an older lady clad in white with a cover over her head walked up to meet us where we were at the far end of the court and when the lady who confronted me saw her, she tried to pretend.

'These girls here refuse to get off the court to let us practise,' she rapidly told her.

'She's trying to lie and says that they practise the whole court. Sound like someone is trying to hog the gym!' I was already fuming with anger, as it appeared they were trying to gang up against us.

The old lady interfered with a sense of maturity and it appeared she was the one in charge here as she spoke with authority in her voice though calmly.

'How about this? You two girls can take the other part of the gym and we will take the other end. Sound fair?' she said as we bargained on the best way to settle all amicably.

As both of us moved toward the other end of the gym, I overheard one of them complain to the old lady. 'Sister Clarence, why did you let them have the other end? You know we normally use the entire gym,' she raised her voice, hissed and spat on the floor to show how disgusted she was. The old lady didn't bother about that as she turned deaf ears to what she was told. She called them to huddle around her while we continued with our workout.

The atmosphere appeared gloomy as the once upon a time a lively team was reduced to a graveyard where silence rules. However, we played one on one on the basketball court without noticing that Sister Clarence and Brittany alongside some other players had been watching us. We seemed to be the equal match as we interchanged position as it required. While I played offence, Khadijah played defence and vice-versa.

Khadijah kept up the ball until I crossed the ball between my legs, confusing Khadijah. I cut the ball one way while making her thought I'd go the other way while slightly bumping her. And I quickly took a three-point shot from a good distance on the court and made it. The onlookers applauded us to our bemusement. Plaudits from the entertained spectators caught our attention and it dawned on me especially that they've been watching us for aeons. I couldn't help but look at Khadijah's face and we beamed a wry smile that carried the insignia: *so we can please our enemies'*. I wiped off the sweat flowing down my hijab, getting ready to go back to serious work-out.

And the team's coach walked over to us trying to talk things out with us. By now, sweats have started dripping down our bodies. She tried to create a sense of familiarity with us. Though we didn't seem cool with that, we still had to give her listening ears.

'I know we got off on the wrong foot the other time but I'd like to move past that,' Sister Clarence spoke to us with a shaky voice.

'I'm quite sure we can,' I replied wiping off the cooling sweat from my face.

Having moved close to us, she sat with us as we panted heavily. She acknowledged our skills and how good we were and paused before she eventually broke the camel's back by proposing to us if we would like to play on the team. We were stunned by that offer.

'Why would you want us to play for you?' Khadijah inquired casting a confused look on her. Sister Clarence went into the details starting from the cause of the sad face the team members wore a few minutes ago. She said they were preparing for the Atlanta City Basketball Tournament during the summer only to be told that they might not be able to compete in the competition. The 'why' behind ruling them out wasn't far-fetched according to Sister Clarence. The rules of the tourney seemed to be against them.

'They've changed a lot of the rules. One of them is that we need ten players. Five plays on the court and five as the reserve. We have to have at least ten registered players,' she said with pain written in her voice.

I dropped my head in my palms trying to figure out what she really wanted from us. Other girls from the team have started coming close by now. And by the time I raised my head from where I buried it, I saw more than half of the team members around me like a prowling lion waiting to devour his prey.

'If you play and our team wins, we can get $5,000. We can split,' Sister Clarence said as she dabbed her face with the helm of his garment.

While I was still deliberating on the proposal from Sister Clarence and my father's non-negotiable rejection, Khadijah gave her upbeat opinion about the offer and the sting from that came like the bee's kiss on an uncovered skin.

'I can't. My dad won't allow me!' I quickly unleashed this outburst which wasn't surprising to Khadijah who knew the extent to which my father can thwart the plan.

'C'mon, I'm quite sure he won't mind for $5,000,' she said confidently. Though my friend said this with confidence, I could still sense from what her face expressed that she was not really sure about the statement she made. I kicked against it bluntly as I spoke on behalf of my father whom I knew would never give his consent.

As we packed our training kits to leave, Sister Clarence handed us the flyer about the tournament and reminded me, should I have a change of thought, the time for the team's practices. Having done that, she walked away while I checked out the flyer dropped in my hand. I checked my watch only to see I am running out of time already.

I whispered to Khadijah's ears the time at the moment. Before she could attempt to encourage me to exercise a little bit of patience, I had already strapped my bag to my back and was walking toward the exit door. At the very instance that I got to the door that leads outside, I felt her from her breath behind me.

All through the journey from Long Island back home, silence took over the journey from us except for the radio in Khadijah's dad's car that was oozing out a country music.

My mind travelled to what my father would say when I tell him. I could hear vividly his voice in my head that 'Never!' and before we could say Jack, we'd arrived home.

3

Back at home, we gathered around the dining table ready to eat immediately after the Maghrib prayer. As usual, different kinds of fruit were arranged on the table. I brought in the last bowl of rice as I joined others.

We engaged ourselves, as usual, in a family talk. And tonight, talk bordered on the fact that my elder brother is at his ripe age for marriage.

'I think it's time that you two got married,' my father broke the news as he lifted the glass of wine on the table to his mouth.

'Dad, I hear you, but I am not ready.' Qadeer, the eldest child of the family, spoke sternly.

'And what makes you think I am ready, Pops? I mean, I just got a job at the High School last fall. I am still getting my feet on the job,' Kasib gave dad his own piece with a wry smile.

Though dad wasn't so pleased with the responses from his two older sons. He felt he should just admonish them. The look that appeared on his face at that moment had not been there for so many years now. It showed all wasn't well at all.

Without being told, he had grown to become a father who had so much to say but has decided to keep to himself more. The reason behind that was best known to him though that never for once hampered his relationship with

25

us as a father. Dad thought a decision shouldn't be made solely outside of Allah.

'Excuses, Excuses! C'mon brothers, everything will all fall into place if you let Allah take control. It'll work out. Just give it some thought,' dad calmly replied them with an unusual laughter written on his lips.

All that my elder brothers could do was to cast a long suspicious look at each other before they allowed laughter escape from their mouth. Immediately my dad's countenance changed slightly and they nodded in agreement to what he had said. And he seemed satisfied with this reaction by smiling coyly and continued eating.

After a moment of silence, I decided to break it with a question for dad. Though my instinct told me he'd be disinterested from the onset, I still worked against my feelings by calling short the long overdue silence which took over our supper.

'Dad, can I…can I talk to you about something?' I stuttered as I spilt out the beans eventually. This was the first time I'd ever feel this way.

'Sure, baby girl. What's on your mind?', dad replied without looking up from his meal. He took an apple, had a bite and cast an inquisitive look on me.

'There's this city basketball tournament in a couple of months and I would like to play if it's….' Dad shut me up abruptly and placed the quarter-apple that was in his right hand on the ceramic plate that rested on the table.

His recent hatred for basketball came to full bloom again as he unapologetically turned the offer down. All efforts to make him reason with me was all to no avail.

'I said no! You are going to focus on something that is more productive as we discussed before. There is no time for basketball.' Though he said this with a ferocious look of a leopard ready to pounce, I could still read his mind that he'd have wanted me to go for that but a fear, I tried to figure to no avail, held him back. Dad made it clear that he had turned his back to basketball and would never rescind his decision.

'It's not fair….,' I sobbed softly and felt an emptiness for the first time in my life.

'I don't care what is fair to you! You're not playing in any tournament. Don't make me regret letting you play basketball at all,' he spat out with anger boldly written on his face. He rose up in annoyance and left for the living room.

My elder brothers tried to ease my pain by appealing to my senses to see reason with dad. I made them understand they really didn't know how it feels like to desire what you found so difficult to have. Life seemed so difficult that I always found myself at the extreme of every situation. With tears rolling down my cheek, I stood up from the table and stormed out of the kitchen and straight to my room.

While I was looking through the flyer that Sister Clarence gave me, checking again the information about the city basketball tournament, I got carried away with the different thoughts that flooded my mind until I was brought back to life with Qadeer's presence in my room. He never visited my room without cause. Thus, I had to turn around and gave him the full attention he required. I gave him a gesture to sit on the bed.

'You know Pops mean well. He just wants what is best for you," he tried to buy me over with his compassionate words.

'So, you agree to what he says about playing basketball?' I asked him to know what he felt about dad's decision. We didn't, for once, ride on the same pedestal. I knew before he entered that his coming might spell another doom. Qadeer, with his long untrimmed beard, had been a good shoulder to lean on. He had always believed in my cause but being a staunched made him advise that I do what I believed within the boundaries of Islam.

As he was talking, I reminisced the time we went with dad to watch mom play a semi-professional basketball game. Then, the craze for basketball in the house was on the top gear level, especially when mom used to make free throws and many a time when mom's three-point shots would save the day for her team.

'You know dad never missed one of mom's game?' He said with conviction in his voice.

'Exactly my point. I don't know why dad won't let me play. I am quite sure Ummi would let me. I should just play without dad knowing!' I spilt out though wasn't afraid of doing that as I trusted Qadeer that he would never betray my trust reposed in him.

'Yeah, you could but…,' Qadeer said but paused in the middle of the phrase and that arrested my attention.

'But what? You're telling me you would snitch on me?' My heart had raced to the finishing line even faster than my shadow when I asked him this. What my mind was processing was if I could just trust him.

I saw in his face when I said that that he agreed with me. His words, which he gave and I swallowed hook, line and sinker, kindled my hopes and aspirations again. I rapidly kissed the red tulip embroidered in my bed sheet and laughed, having seen a shoulder I could at least lean on. In the course of our heart-to-heart discussion, dad suddenly called the adhan for Isha prayer. The call to prayer made us stop our talk abruptly.

'Hurry up and make Wudu. You know how dad hates for us to be late for prayers.' He made his way towards the door and as he opened the door, he looked back at me for the last time, smiled and left.

For years, dad had been the one leading the prayer. While Kasib and Qadeer would stand behind him shoulder to shoulder, I always kept my distance behind everybody as I followed through their motions during the prayer.

The next day, Khadijah and I made our way to the Long Island Catholic Community Center after school hours. And as we walked into the gym where the Ladies of Faith were getting ready to perform their routine warm up and practice, Sister Clarence was stunned seeing us.

Khadijah wore a personal made white basketball jersey, with a black cat-suit underneath to cover her skin and a matching hijab. I wore a jogging suit with a hijab, which I tucked my good luck red tulip that I plucked from my personal garden before leaving the house in the morning. Sister Clarence smiled as she flung her hands wide to embrace us.

'I'm glad you two have made it.' I apologized for making us arrive behind the scheduled time. She never made any fuss about that.

Having embraced the team's coach, we walked on the court and a few of the team welcomed us warmly. Our presence was still greeted with some levels of coldness from some members of the team who went to gossip about our presence. One of the girls chuckled from where they sat in cliques and nobody had to tell me that they were really talking about us. I also noticed they were making snide remarks about us with the way they were looking at us and laughing hysterically.

About twenty minutes later, after we'd changed into our practice gear, Sister Clarence started the practice. She put us through a series of basketball drills and reeled out some coaching directions. The jogging pant she wore made her look smart though with a cover over her head. We went on hustling up on the court.

During this practice, another lady of Sister Clarence's kind walked into the gym and approached our coach. From what the ladies were saying, she oversees the community centre's affairs. Sister Harry, as she was called, was a plump lady with a rickety walking step.

'Excuse me, Sister Clarence, can I talk to you for a moment?' Her husky voice echoed in the gym. With that, few of the ladies bemused with a smile while some others couldn't hold themselves but to laugh so loud. After whispering to Sister Clarence's ears, she turned back to leave. Then, coach summoned Brittany to come off the court and on to the sidelines with her. All we saw from afar were moving lips and hands outstretched towards our direction. We were wondering what could be wrong that we were kept in the dark this way.

Different thoughts began flashing like lightning in me. As we were practising, my mind went back to my dad's tone of finality regarding the rejection. Brittany came back moments later to roll out some instructions passed down from our coach. The way she was conducting the build-up, I could sense strongly that there were some of the orders which were hers. Every member of her cliques was preferentially treated.

'Could I have been the reason for the emergency invitation by the Ladies of Faith administrator?' I asked myself. My mind had travelled farther than my imagination. All that Brittany was doing wasn't in any way thrilling to me. My mind was with Sister Clarence because since Sister Harry had come to call her, we've never heard anything from within nor saw any of them walk into that room.

****

'I called you in so that Father and I can discuss your new recruits for the team.' Sister Harris spoke vehemently. Sister Clarence inquired about the wrongdoings in what she had done.

'Sister Harris has concerns about your recruiting tactics that were abrupt.' Father McGinnis, who was just transferred to the district, was also in attendance.

Sister Clarence, having been briefed of their plan to let go of the new recruits because they are Muslims, had a change of countenance to that of a fiery-looking ember.

'You are asking me to kick our new players off the team because they are Muslims? I am afraid we can't do that.' She gave them the piece of her mind. Father McGinnis was brought over by Sister Clarence's parable and was convinced too that the new recruits should stay.

'Sister Clarence is trying to say that if we remove these girls from the team because they are Muslims, it could lead to a lawsuit. We don't want that to happen. Besides, I don't see what harm it could do to allow these girls to play.' After saying that, he looked at his watch, got off the chair and left the office to excuse himself as he had a golf game to watch.

****

Moments later, I saw Sister Clarence appear from the room she was invited into twenty minutes ago. Though we were still conducting practice, the enthusiasm in doing that was never there. Her sullen look as she got nearer and nearer said it all, that all was not well.

Some selected few among the girls stood in twos to pass snide remarks which came in form of murmurings and grumblings. I hardly got wind of what they were saying even though I had the conviction that we were their centre of discussion as all eyes were feasting on our bodies.

After rejoining the team, she called members of the squad together to further increase the tempo of our practice. According to her selections, three girls were to a team. Khadijah was teamed up Joanna and Henrietta, while unfortunately I was teamed up with Nancy and Jenny. From this selection, I was expecting nothing short of cold attitude.

Sister Clarence and the team's skipper, Brittany, having packed neatly her blonde hair, sat on the sidelines as they observed the players. In my team, we joggled the ball among us to establish trust.

We did quite a lot of workouts and the look on her face when she got back to our midst changed to that of a new child with innocence beaming on its lips. A few minutes later, the whistle went off, signalling the end of the practice. My annoyance was immediately registered.

'What was that? I was open for the pass,' I tried to iron it out with Nancy who was on the team with me.

'I saw I had the shot so I took it,' she snobbishly responded as she was packing up her clothes.

'What are you talking about? You were not open at all.' I tried to talk things out with her as I laced up my sneakers.

'Look, you don't like how I play? You can get off the team.' She gave me her piece which stung me like a bee's sting and she walked away.

While this was going on, everybody had hustled and surrounded the coach for an announcement. I had to quickly join to not be left out. Sister Clarence took her time, while she was adjusting the cover on her head, to commend everybody's efforts. However, she never failed to say that my group should work out our differences. Nancy never allowed that to be cold before whipping me with her eyes from my head to toe.

Having gone through the basics of the training and the need for us to trust one another which could make us get the result, Sister Clarence opened her clipboard and removed copies of the summer city basketball schedule.

'Listen up ladies. I have received the basketball schedule for the city tournaments. Our first game is in a month,' she said as she passed out the schedule to other members of the team. We knew that having the schedule wouldn't guarantee our featuring in the competition because as it stood, we didn't have ten players on the team yet. The manner of faith exercised by the coach, I had not seen before. And that took me to remember that one of the strongest pillars of Islam is the belief in Allah. In no time, she dismissed the practice.

Just as Khadijah and I walked out of the gym, we were called over by Sister Clarence. We had to stay behind as the other team member vacated the gym. At this moment, I told my thought that I'd already said. A thought dropped into my heart, making me believe that we would be thrown-off the team, the outcome of the clandestine was the meeting she went to have with Sister Harry.

'Two things: one, your uniforms and registration for the city tournament. We need \$50 to get your uniforms made and \$50 to register you in the tournament,' she said emphatically and looked as though she was reading it out from the pamphlet with her. Though this caught me unaware, I was still not satiated as I still think the other 'thing' would definitely be about our admission, considering our mode of dressing which was different from others. I never allowed that to rest.

'What is the other thing you need to talk to us about?' I rushed the words out of my mouth while checking the time so as not to get home after my dad had settled in. Should that by chance happen, he would do nothing but ask in plain what kept me out so late. So, I was expecting our coach to spill out the beans for me to just leave and go and moan for my mattress.

'As you just heard, we still need two more players. Could you two ask around and see if you can get two more recruits?' As she said this in a soft tone, it appeared I just had a chilly bath in a jacuzzi. Since the matters of discourse were different from what troubled my mind, though still unconvinced, I assured the coach of our profound support before we made our way out of the gym.

In the cool of the evening, my dad was reading the newspaper while Qadeer was watching TV as his usual practice. The day seemed bright today as the weather spoke in a friendly manner. As I walked into the living room with a sore limp, Qadeer took notice and slightly chuckled.

From what I saw, my dad was fully engrossed in the newspaper in his hands. Nothing enticed me in the dailies because no day will go by without reporting an incident of a Muslim girl that was mobbed by some angry white folks.

Early last year, I couldn't go to school because of the curfew resulting from the tragic loss of a Muslim teenage girl, whose body was found beside the canal after seven days of search. And when the result of her autopsy came out, she died after being strangled. Blood stains were found, according to reports, dripping from her laps. The curfew lasted for two weeks before the air was cleared for us to return to school. My mind came back letting me know where I am. As I drew the attention of my dad to myself, he put down the newspaper raised towards his face.

'I need $200,' I swiftly poured out the words out. Father wore a suspicious look on his face though I knew quite alright that he never had a cause to disbelieve me for once since I never gave him room to doubt me.

'Khadijah and I are going shopping for some abayas and hijabs that are comfortable for the summer,' I quickly added without giving him any room to doubt me. He never thought about it twice. So, I felt elated within me that I had won over with my first-time lie to one of the men in my life but not so sure if the other man who was there was bought over at all with the way he looked at me from his left-side eye.

And moments later, it was confirmed that I could only fool my father. I was in bed going through a science book and was so deep in my study as music played through my headphones from my smartphone. Qadeer startled me after he tapped me on the shoulders.

'Hey, don't sneak up on me like that!' I told him as I quickly turned around.

'Sorry, I didn't mean to startle you,' he said apologetically and moved forward to sit. I was still wondering why he was in my room at that moment. It later dawned on me that all I thought I was covering was not hidden at all.

'So, how did it go?', he asked with an inquisitive look on his face.

'How did what go?' I tried to feign ignorance.

'Your first practice.' Qadeer continued to play along too, with a childish smile appearing on his face.

'I don't know what you are talking about.' I was feeling within, how on earth did he know I had gone for the practice?

'You know exactly what I am talking about. C'mon sis, you don't have to be that way with me. I know you joined that team already. The sore muscle limp. You walked into the living room like anybody that had their muscles worked.' My eyes widened out as I was shocked at how I easily sold myself out when I thought I could keep it a secret easily. As it stood, I couldn't deny again. I told him to shut the door behind him.

'Practice was awesome. There are a few girls that have a problem with me but there's nothing I can't handle.' I took him through the routine of the day. I did not fail to make him know of the team's challenges at the moment and having heard that, he offered to be of assistance.

'I know the coach at my high school for the basketball team. Maybe I can ask him to see if there could be players that might be interested in playing for your team,' he said it with a look that told me, without any iota of doubt, that he would do it.

Qadeer also told me of father's arrangement of a sister for him after he had calmed my nerves down that he'd provide the needed support for me with regards to my passion. I became curious about touching whom he'd plan to meet.

'Whoa! One question at a time. Her name is Ameera Williams. She's nice and that's what I can tell so far. Coincidentally, she works at the high school,' he said with confidence written in his tone.

His look spoke contrarily to what he just divulged as if he wasn't in any way happy. Life offered him a lot of chances. I rose-up to shut the window blind, preventing the raging wind from scattering the books on the table. Minutes later, he stood up and left the room. I felt relaxed that at least someone in the house believed in my cause.

4

The Manhattan Community Center was filled to the brim that hardly could the spectators' breaths be heard. All the strands of hair of the people who graced the opening session of this tournament were on both ends.

From the outset, the referee was going to disqualify the Muslim players who wore leggings and long sleeves under their uniforms as well as the hijab. The ever-resilient Sister Clarence fought the ruling as she claimed that it would be discrimination. After much talk, they were given the green to play as they were.

As it stood in the fourth quarter, with one minute and twenty-three seconds left, the Ladies of Faith weren't doing really well in the clash against the Manhattan Bobcats because they lacked teamwork amongst themselves. The score stood 57-49. Sister Clarence wasn't too pleased with this as she felt so disappointed with Jenny, who decided to set aside the Muslim players in the team out of sheer hatred for the women of the cloth.

'C'mon you know better to make a pass like that!' Sister Clarence screamed out at Jenny and flung the book in her to a side.

Moments later, Nadeera, with her Red Tulip tucked on her jersey, took hold of the ball, dribbled it down the court, passed it to Khadijah, who sped it up court then sent it flying back to Nadeera. And when Nadeera saw that

Brittany was open, she quickly passed it to her, who saw an opening for a shot which she took.

Though she missed the shot, the day was saved by Nadeera who laid the ball up and made the shot, recording the score now 60-51. That brought a smile to Sister Clarence's face.

'Good job ladies!' She jumped up as she punched the air simultaneously.

Little had that tumultuous joy die down that the other team repossessed the ball. She passed the ball to her other team players and as she tried to force it up the court, the ball was brilliantly stolen by Khadijah, who in turn passed it to Nancy. After Nancy took the ball and forced it up the court, her attempt to shoot the ball was neatly blocked by the other team player.

Everybody could feel the intensity of the game. There were falls, defensive skills, and offensive adroitness. Another team player from the opposite side rushed the ball up court. Though Nadeera guarded the opponent diligently, the team player tried all she could to shake Nadeera, and when she failed to watch her hand coordination with the ball, Nadeera wittingly stole the ball from her, went for the shot and made it.

However, that wasn't enough to secure the day for the Ladies of Faith as the timer on the game clock had run out. While the other team celebrated their victory, the Ladies of Faith looked dejected. All through the time, that disappointment was boldly written on their faces. Sister Clarence held her composure as she was upset by the gameplay of a few players. She called the ladies together.

Ten minutes later, the Ladies of Faith walked into the gym with the soles of their feet stealthily treading upon the face of the earth. Sister Clarence entered almost immediately and her face said it all that all wasn't well, following the disappointing outing.

'First of all, I would like to commend those who played a good game. Majority of you all showed a good cohesion of teamwork. Now, for those who decided to do what they wanted to do on the court, I have a problem,' she said with anger accompanying her post-match address.

'Those, who chose to ball hog and refuse to pass it to their teammates showed that there is a lack of trust and most of all, lack of maturity. I guarantee you I'm going to work you all until we all get it.' She called it a day with the team and left them without any further instructions.

On Monday afternoon, the Ladies of Faith were seen running laps for the majority of their practice after having had a disappointing outing at the Manhattan Community Center. With what they were doing, it appeared suicidal. Though they seemed fagged out having done thirty runs, they still had thirty more to go.

'I don't like making you run but this is necessary. Yes, this is punishment, but this will also help you. So, c'mon push it, ladies!', she pityingly screamed at them while they continued their drills.

Exhaustion was written on their faces as they continued with their push-ups. They were also practising some blocking drills. Sister Clarence felt she should put a stop to the drills but her look contradicted her feelings and she had nothing to do but to succumb to what her look was saying.

Eventually, they got to the last phase of their practice. And while they were still practising in their uniforms, they sparred off. Sister Clarence beamed a smile. She almost applauded them when she saw attitudes changing in Nancy and Jenny, who passed the ball to their Muslim teammates.

After getting the satisfaction she desired to see, the coach blew her whistle, signalling the end of the practice. The ladies, with fatigue in their bodies, grabbed their bags and walked out of the gym sluggishly.

'Alright ladies, that will be it for the day. See you all at practice tomorrow.' She dismissed the ladies who felt a huge relief as they headed to the exit door.

Sister Clarence sat in a meditative mood in her office grading the papers. And as she saw a grade, she wasn't really proud of by one of her students. Just as she finished grading the paper, a knock took her eyes off grading papers for the first time. A concerned look was written on the face of Brittany as she entered Sister Clarence's office and that got the coach worried. Brittany, wearing the look as if she wanted to say something, walked in and took a seat.

'I was thinking. I think we should not start Joanna and Nancy tomorrow,' she said while looking straight into the house of the coach and that got Sister Clarence startled.

Brittany went on with confidence written in her voice: 'It's just that the new team members have done an excellent job in the past two games and I think we really could win the next game with a major lead if we start our new team members.'

'I can't do that!' Sister Clarence replied to her profoundly with a shrink forming a bridge across her face. Brittany's inquisitive look got her talking further.

'Well for one, the girls have seniority on the team. They have been on the team for three years. You know that!' The coach said that convincingly but that really didn't bother Brittany, which wasn't to the amazement of Sister Clarence. Brittany felt having the seniors start may not guarantee them another victory.

'There is no such thing as a no-guaranteed win. What you're asking is not fear. You have to understand that winning is not everything. Yes, we need money but not to the point when you're out with your friends to get it.' The coach said this unapologetically but it didn't bulge Brittany, not even an inch.

'So what? Are we just supposed to lose? You know that we need to work on our defence and need to practice our free throws. We could really win.' Desperation was written in Brittany's voice as she poured out her mind.

'And what would it matter if a man gains the whole world and lose his soul? Well, in your case, your friends? Brittany, have faith that everything will work out. If we lose, God is still good.' The preaching nature of Sister Clarence took the scene but to her surprise, Brittany wasn't moved though she had to succumb to the coach's admonitions.

'As I said God is still good. Now, go home, get a good night's rest and we will have fun on the court tomorrow, regardless that we would win or lose.' She stood up as she patted Brittany on her back. In a sad and frustrated manner, Brittany nodded in agreement, got up out of her seat and headed for the office door.

As I walked into the house with my duffle bag hung over my shoulders, what I saw stole my heart. Kasib was casually dressed as with a kufi and appeared upset with me as his eyes were brewing fire on sighting me. I wanted to quickly tell him something to cover up my track after he had inquired to know my whereabouts.

'I was with Khadijah and some friends. What's wrong with you?' I told him without a second thought in a defensive manner.

'Have you forgotten that we are having dinner with the two sisters and their wali tonight?', he looked me straight in the eyes and asked. I got so carried away with the city basketball tournament that I forgot we were supposed to entertain some guests. I never believed it could be so quick, hence, I offered to get things done on time before the guests' arrival. I dropped my duffle bag in front of my room before I headed straight to the kitchen.

The two families sat behind the dining table to have a healthy meal in their quietness. After the meal, my dad and Mr. Shaheed discussed the marriage contract. Everybody's attention was given to the conversation except me. While others gave their ears to the contract discussion, I hid my phone underneath which I used to text Khadijah.

I saw Mr. Shaheed hand my dad the marriage contract. My father read it aloud. I barely heard what he read since my mind wasn't there at all. Having read it, other people's mumbling comments drew my attention to see that my dad had passed the contract to my brothers. My chuckling was wrongly timed, having seen a text with a picture sent by Khadijah to me. My father smartly cut me a look.

After all the guests had left and Qadeer and Kasib had gone to bed for work, I went straight to the kitchen to wash the dishes. While that was going on, my dad walked into the kitchen to help to dry the dishes. Anytime my dad wanted to squeeze out some piece of information from you, he'd become so close that you wouldn't know when you will start letting the cat out of your bag. Both of us took a seat at the kitchen table after drying the dishes.

'I have been thinking. In two years, you'll be graduating and going off to college. I think it will be best that you should get married,' my dad spoke sternly, burying his head in the newspaper with him. This came as shocking news to me and I couldn't figure out what we could do in this situation. Dad took me through the plan of what he discussed with Mr. Shaheed about my marriage proposal.

'Brother Shaheed has a nephew about your age. He has the same goals as you. We figure that you two could get married and go to college together,' dad spoke to me in a lighter mood.

My look was still surprised as I kept imagining what our guest saw in me that made him request for my hand in marriage for his nephew. I placed my head on the table and all that was left was my thoughts waging war with my feelings.

'Just give it some thought. Maybe if you meet the brother, it will be quite clear,' he spoke with a little smile beaming from his lips. My thoughts kept calling on me to give it a thought.

The meeting between Brother Shaheed Hassan's nephew, Fuquan Hassan and I was scheduled to take place at the park. We eventually met up at a park bench as the rendezvous point. When I gazed at Fuquan, he seemed very attractive with a cherry brown skin tone. Though he had a little acne, his lightly grown and trimmed goatee made up for it. Not to mention the glasses he wore which gave him a geeky look. I had always found men who wore glasses attractive. I quickly lowered my gaze to keep my piety safe-guarded.

In no time, we struck up a generic conversation as we were getting to know each other. By now, we had entered the basketball court. Fuguan took a shot and made the basket. I grabbed the ball and dribble it around, took some shots and made them.

When we later met that afternoon at Halal Restaurant after the series of layups we had done in the gym, both of us poured out our hearts. And when I narrated my ordeal in the hands of my father with regards to choice, he admonished me as though we've known for ages.

'I am part of a basketball team,' I said, hoping to hear out his opinion on the matter on the ground. Fuquan gave his sincere view about my passion which made my interest in him waxed stronger and stronger. I watched him as he took a bite of his fries. And he went on to inquire about the team which I was playing for. With the ensued conversation, my fondness for him appeared on the high side. He gave his word to come to see my next game. Nightfall beckoned on us and we hearkened to its voice.

****

Prior to our practice the next day, the same way I was stunned when I heard the proposal from my dad was the same way Khadijah felt. And without causing any other confusion, I quickly told them as Sister Clarence had started walking towards the gym this time that it was a long-term plan.

Khadijah smiled shyly having heard that. Our practice was impressive as we began to learn how to cooperate with one another. It was a light practice for us to have time to relax our nerves before the D-day.

****

A lot of people, by now, were waiting outside on queue to pay for their admission into the Queens Community Gym, as it was another game night for the Ladies of Faith who would be playing against the Queensboro Queens.

Undoubtedly, this time around, the Ladies of Faith were having a good game here as they took the lead of 73-62 and the clock read 2 minutes and 27 seconds. All hands were on deck at the moment to secure the victory for the team.

Nadeera kissed her good luck charm- the Red Tulip, who had been impressive all day, took the three-point shot and scored the basket. Caught among the spectators was Fuquan, rooting for the Ladies of Faith. With the clock soon to dry up in the fourth quarter, the Ladies of Faith continued their dominance over their rivals. And when the buzzer finally went off, the Ladies of Faith celebrated their victory and some of their faithful couldn't contain their joy as they ran to the court to embrace some of the players.

Later that evening, the team made their way to the gym. They seemed to be in good spirit as they were still in the euphoria of their victory. Brittany and some selected few decided to mark it by going out on a date at a café sharing a gourmet Mediterranean pizza while they talked about the game.

After a fun-filled day of hanging out with my teammates, I walked into the house delightsomely and humming a song. And as I made my way to the kitchen, my dad called me to the living room. The state in which I met my dad, Qadeer and Kasib was not pleasant at all. Could it be another tragedy from the family? Except for these people on the seat, dad never told us of any other family members. So, why was there a tensed atmosphere?

While I was still wondering what could have gone wrong, I saw my basketball uniform stretched out on the table and immediately a nervous chilled sweat ran down my spine to my bladder. Both of brothers were excused from the room. Then I knew a doom is about to boomerang as he never excused them from matters relating to any of us before. He broke the silence.

'By the way you eyeballed the uniform on the table, you know what's going on,' he spoke with the tenacity that I couldn't figure out when I saw him in this state. When I tried to offer an explanation for all that happened, my father got upset the more. I had already anticipated for an event turn-out like this before but never knew it could be this rapid. All we could hear in the house was his voice.

'Go on! Explain how you disobeyed me when I clearly told you that I did not want you to play basketball!' His anger was triggered in a way that I felt so insecure with him for the first time in about 16 years. I felt he was annoyed because he thought I chose basketball over Allah.

'I didn't. I mean, Allah has given me the skills and abilities to play! Do you remember how he blessed Ummi...,' I said thoughtfully thinking I was proving a point.

'Leave your mother out of this! You are done playing. Wallahi, if I see or even hear you on any basketball court in this city, you will regret it!' He gave his verdict, while tears strolled down my cheeks, grabbed the uniform and walked out of the living room.

I stood there shaken visibly by father's outburst. The tears, by now, were forming pathways on my face. Never for once have I seen him in this state. He must have hated basketball with a passion to have cut short my dream. My legs failed me as they could only manage to carry me to my room where I sobbed loudly to my waiting pillows.

When I heard footsteps towards the kitchen, I pulled down the clothes in my wardrobe to be able to hear what

those legs in the kitchen would be saying any moment
soon. My dad was mumbling in frustration.

'I really think you should give her a chance to play.
Nadeera has skills.' Qadeer threw his weight of support
behind me and that cooled my boiling body temperature at
the moment.

'Yeah, so does every girl her age who thinks they can
play professionally. What do you think is going to happen
if she does not make it to the pros just as she hopes? The
best thing for her is to concentrate on those books and
Islam,' he spoke sternly.

And while Qadeer was trying to convince dad, he
mistakenly spilt out the beans about knowing that I was
playing. His anger got rekindled. Dad was just rolling out
brimstones and fire from under his belly and I came to a
conclusion that hell has got no fury like what was going on
in the house.

'You got that right. When you get kids of your own,
you can raise them any way you want. Stop trying to raise
mine!' Dad vomited his last venom before storming out of
the kitchen.

I just retired to my bed and picked my phone to talk to
Fuquan about my dad's ban from playing basketball.

'I don't understand why my dad is losing his mind
about me playing basketball. It's something I want to do.'
My voice was shaking as I tried to express my anger at
what was contrary to my passion.

'I don't see why he won't let you play. Sister, you're
good. If you were my wife, I would let you play as much as

you want. You have mad skills.' Fuquan's statement brought out the smile slightly from my mouth. At the very instance that I doubted his praising of me, he quickly reverted:

'Trust me. You play way better than half the brothers I know at my Masjid. What do you see yourself doing with your skills?', he asked suddenly and that caught me off-guard.

'Well, I want to play in the WNBA as my mom did. I just don't know how that is going to work. I don't even have a college recruiter scouting me at this point to even play for college.' I never knew when I spilt this out of my mouth, but I became so familiar with Fuquan as he brought out the life in me.

Though I was upset with how I was being treated that I almost planned to uproot the flower I cherished most in my life, the emotional support and advice I got from Fuquan, at least, lightened the mood. He also invited me to a poetry night at the Starbucks café. Minutes later, dad opened my door suddenly to invite me to the living room to hear some good news from my elder brothers.

'Kasib and I have good news to share,' Qadeer set the ball rolling though he spoke softly.

'We have decided that we are getting married to the two sisters!' Kasib spoke excitedly.

While the joy became infectious immediately, I still felt cheated as I was robbed in a broad daylight what would have given me the kind of joy others were sharing. I could not make it known that I wasn't happy with that.

And as soon as I retired to bed for the day, I felt emptiness, strong enough to push up scorpions into my heads, in my bowel. And every day, I waited a day when my dream will eventually be fulfilled and my Red Tulip will blossom brightly as I kept watering.

My friends accompanied me to an Islamic store to shop for an abaya for poetry night. I picked out a few to try on. We were inside the store checking out abayas and Khimars. Brittany also came along to feed her eyes.

As I tried on various abayas of the dresses and looked at myself in the mirror, Khadijah and Brittany gave their approval and disapproval at every interval. Brittany was fascinated by the beauty of the clothes as she picked up an abaya and placed it on her body, observing herself in the mirror. Later, Brittany entered the dressing room to try one of the abayas on and she got the compliments.

'I don't think I should get this. I am not Muslim and I can't afford it,' Brittany reacted to our compliments naughtily.

'You don't have to be Muslim to wear an abaya. And two, if you want it, I will get it for you.' I assured her it would be a gift from me to her.

5

Since the day of my ban, my dad never left me behind at home. He would call me from my room each time he got ready to leave the house. And I had to rush out of my room and make my way out of the house. My dad followed me out the door as we made our way into the car.

Reluctantly, I would step out of the car after he had pulled up in front of the Masjid. It was not because my father had to make me go to Islamic study class but because he banned me from playing basketball.

'Why the long face? Give it a chance. You will like it.' He tried to calm my nerves having seen the look on my face.

'I don't have a problem going to Haliqa classes. It's just that…do I really have to quit basketball?' I tried to be reasonable with him with my apologetic look.

'Yes, and my decision is final! It's best that you get inside before class start without you,' he said with a tone of finality and turned the ignition. He revved the car and zoomed off speedily.

Four hours later, as I walked out of the Masjid, I saw my dad's car already waiting outside for me. I took no second thought before I walked towards the parked car and got in. Dad tried to be friendly as he smiled at me. I couldn't help but force a smile on my face. Before we followed the route back home, we stopped by a restaurant to satiate my hunger.

Some days later, after an afternoon Haliqa class, I met with Khadijah as we were heading home. She told me of her meeting with a few of the team members. I could still sense that they still longed for me but I rejected the offer.

'I can't because I have to meet up with my brothers' fiancées to try on wedding abayas. Tell them I said hello and congratulations on their wins.' I felt a strong potion of scorpion's poisonous sting was pushed down my throat to have been forcefully left out of the team's success.

Khadijah tried all she could to convince me to go out with them until I hesitantly gave in to her demand. I could see written on her face the joy that I would be spending my next hour with the team. With the way she reacted, she seemed to have been waiting for a day like this.

Moments later, we were gathered in a corner booth of the café. My ban was the subject of discourse here.

'You telling me that your dad won't let you play. Why not? He has to know how good you are,' Brittany set the room ablaze.

'Her dad is very strict. I am lucky to even get to see her at the Masjid,' Khadijah added her voice, though it bothered me not.

'I know your dad probably means well but you have to do what you feel is right for you.' Henrietta offered an alternative option which I had done once but got me where I stood now.

'Don't encourage her to disobey her dad. She has gotten into enough trouble as it is.' Rahima, one of the newest Muslim players, also offered a shoulder to lean on but none could understand me.

I was not there with them mentally as I was thinking about how the joy written on all of their faces could have been mine. When it appeared that I was the reason for gathering, I quickly called it to quit.

'Enough about my problems. How is the rest of the team doing?' I asked to lighten up the atmosphere a little bit. The team made it to the top playoffs. Though I was happy for them which I couldn't conceal, my disappointment was in myself that I wasn't part of that success story. An attempt was made by Brittany to go back to my story. I had to change the subject since it was hard for me to talk about my passion that I wasn't allowed to pursue.

My marriage arrangement with Fuquan was brought up and when I tried to shove it aside, I was challenged immediately by the albino in our midst, Rahima. I also let them know what the arrangement was as against what they thought. While this talk was ongoing, my ringtone went off. As I looked through my phone, I told them it was time to leave. Khadijah and I got up from where we sat and left the café. And a few minutes later, I was relaxing in Khadijah's car as we journeyed back home.

On a Thursday afternoon, I was at home cooking food in preparation for my two brothers' wedding. As soon as I finished seasoning the food and put the food in the oven, the doorbell rang. My father shouted from upstairs alerting anybody nearby to go get the door. I rushed to the living room to get the door, having covered my head with an abaya. When I turned the doorknob to open, the figure standing before me left my mouth ajar.

'Sister Clarence, what are you doing here?' I asked with puzzlement on my face.

'I was in the neighbourhood and I thought I would stop by and see how you are doing,' she said while she expected I asked her to come in.

Since she was not privy to the decision that my dad had disallowed me from any basketball-related activities, she tried to inquire why I've not been on the ground for practice. We were still in the middle of our discussion when my dad suddenly came to the door dressed in a loose shirt, pant, and kufi.

'I am Sister Clarence. I am Nadeera's coach. I have stopped by to see if Nadeera will be coming to practice later on today.' She spoke with the kind of confidence that you find unusual among women of my kind, especially to a man.

'I am sorry that she did not tell you but we decided that she won't be playing basketball anymore.' My father's words, showing strictness, stung me again and I was almost driven to tears.

After Sister Clarence had walked away from the door, my father shut the door behind him. I looked at him this time around to show that I disagreed with how he treated Sister Clarence. The look of contempt caught the attention of my dad.

'I know what you are thinking. You have to understand that life is more than bouncing and shooting a ball on the court.' He spoke softly to me this time as he flung his arm around my shoulder.

Later that day, as I was emptying the closet and removing old coats that were not worn in years, I saw a few boxes that were sealed. As I was removing them one by one, I came across a box with the label *Jameela's Stuff*. I stared at the box that held captive my mother's possessions.

Without much ado, I quickly peeled off the label and opened it. I saw basketball trophies with my mother's name as MVP. The anticipatory look on my face made me continue to dig through the box until I came across pictures of my mother being on the basketball team. I never stopped digging through the box until I saw my handsome dad in a basketball uniform hugged up with my mom wearing the same uniform. I turned the picture around only to see the word saying *"Together forever…Always!"*

Tears slightly strolled down my cheeks as I looked at the picture to see how happy my dad looked in the picture. I never for once saw him smile this way since Ummi, my mother, died. I felt I needed to find out why the sudden change.

After some hours, my dad walked into the house after what seemed to be a long day of work as fatigue could be seen all over his body. He walked into the living room only to see that I sat on the couch with the box of my mother's sports memorabilia.

He took a long look at the box and said he could remember that he taped the box. One thing he detested is for his child to do less or more than his bidding. I knew he would be triggered to anger today again because I did more than he had sent me to do but I quickly told him what prompted that.

'I could not help it! It had mom's name on it. Dad, mom played basketball and you were totally fine with it. I even found this picture.' I handed him the picture thinking it would soften his heart.

'Enough! I don't want to talk about this anymore!' He grabbed the box from me and stormed out of the living room while I just sighed.

****

At the reception in the hotel banquet hall where the married couples rented for their reception, the couples sat at the bride and groom table. The banquet hall was filled with Muslims. The guests invited sat at the tables that were decorated with fancy silverware and tablecloth as well as dinner napkins the same colours as the wedding theme colours.

While the merriment was ongoing inside the hall, I sat in a chair in the hallway as I scrolled through the pictures of the Ladies of Faith basketball team. Qadeer was few metres away from me.

'May I sit here?', he asked me as he took a seat across from me in a matching chair.

'It's your wedding day. You have every right to sit here.' I slightly giggled.

He talked me through my thought about the game tonight. I admitted that was what brought me out but couldn't help the situation. He offered to be of help.

'Listen to me; you know I always told you that I supported whatever you do. I always told you to obey dad because I understand the man that he is. He may be strict but he loves you. Now, I am telling you to go get what you want. Go play tonight.' His words to me were the nicest things I have ever heard in my life since birth.

Amatullah suddenly walked out of the hallway to call Qadeer for a photo session as soon as he finished giving me his words and backings. He got up from his seat and locked arms with his wife as they walked back into the banquet hall. I stood there to ponder for a second before calling Khadijah.

'Hello, Khadijah!' I hung the phone after getting the response from the other end.

EPILOGUE

The big guns, as well as the small fry in the society, were lining up as they pay for their tickets at the door. In the Ladies' of Faith locker room at the Mt. Vernon Community Center, the team players were preparing for their final game of the summer. Sister Clarence gave her last words prior to the contest.

'Alright, ladies. Big day for all of us. I know we have pressure to win the cash prize but let's not focus on that. I want you ladies to have fun,' she said with positive vibes written in her voice and on her face. And as we walked into the locker room, the excitement from Sister Clarence and our teammates was massive. The coach walked up to me with an open embrace to show how excited she was but also to quickly tell me I would feature for the team in the second half.

Both teams have stepped out on the court for the clash. The Ladies of Faith and the Mt. Vernon Valkyries were in the middle of the court for tip-off. The referee threw the ball in the air which was won by one of the team members from the Valkyries.

An hour and a half later, it was the second half of the game and the Ladies of Faith were losing the game 67-59 with just 20 seconds before the end of the third quarter of the game. The Mt. Vernon Valkyries were in possession of the ball.

Jersey number 23 passed the ball to number 34 who pushed the ball to the other end of the court. Rahima attempted to steal the ball but failed despite all her antics. Jersey number 53 shot a three-pointer and she made it. The spectators cheered as the clock buzzer went off signalling the end of the quarter. Each team went to their respected sides. Sister Clarence, as usual, called her team into her side.

While this was going on, Nadeera's dad, Bilal, had just arrived at the entrance of the community centre. His entire attempt to enter forcefully proved abortive. He tried all he could to push past the security officer but he was stopped once again. And having paid $10, he was allowed inside.

Immediately he entered. He was still searching to see Nadeera when he saw Fuquan. He made his way to mid-sections where Fuquan sat. After letting Fuquan in on his mission, he later calmed his nerves as he felt that Fuquan had a point.

'Well, it sounds better to sit and watch her play than being kicked out by security,' Fuquan had earlier admonished him.

The fourth quarter started and it was the Ladies of Faith ball. Khadijah was underneath the Valkyries goal. She passed the ball to Brittany and the latter pushed the ball before sending it to Ayeesha. And when Ayeesha got the ball, she ran the ball to half court and then passed it to Nadeera who pushed it to the three-point line. Following Nadeera's fancy footwork and dribbling which got her opponent confused, she pretended to go one direction but went the other leaving her guard behind. Nadeera took a three-point shot and made it. That amazed her dad where he was sitting.

A Valkyrie player, with jersey number 42 possessed the ball and passed it to jersey number 78, who pushed the ball down court. Her pass was intercepted by Nadeera, who forced the ball down the other end of the court. Bilal's daughter passed the ball to Brittany who pushed the ball into two-point range, took the shot and made it.

With 30 seconds left in the game, the Valkyries still had a five-point lead. Sister Clarence called for a time-out and her team members quickly huddled around her.

'Alright, we are still in the game. It's our ball. I want Nadeera to get the ball. I want you to make two three-point shots. Once Nadeera makes the shot and the ball is in the Valkyries' possession, ladies, steal the ball at all cost. And once you get the ball, pass it to Nadeera for another three-point shot. Got it?' She reeled out her last order to the ladies and the team confirmed in unison.

Both teams hustled back on to the court. Ayeesha took possession of the ball to the sidelines on their side and passed the ball to Henrietta, who found a hole in the opponents' defence despite their heavy protection and passed the ball to Nadeera, who went for a three-point shot and made it.

The clock buzzer went off, signalling the end of the game after Nadeera's last attempt for a three-point shot was blocked. While the Valkyrie team cheered as they won the game, the Ladies of Faith wore a defeated look on their faces but Sister Clarence quickly called her team to the sideline in order to shake hands with the winners.

Minutes later, as I walked out with my team talking with them, the voice that I heard call me surprised me. I looked up with fear on my face as I turned to see my dad with an emotionless look. I was left with my dad to talk things out. Immediately I left. I couldn't contain my fear again.

'Dad, I know I disobeyed you but I had to. This is something I wanted to do. Ummi loved basketball and you did too once in your life. Why can't I play? I understand if you don't forgive me for this but I am going to keep playing even if I have to move out of the house,' I said with my head bowed.

My father's silence worsened the situation the more and I felt at the moment that the earth should just open up its bowel and swallow me up. It got me confused the more.

Eventually, when he opened his mouth to talk, it was just a whole lot of confession from him.

'You played more than good. You were awesome out there. I guess you have a lot of your mom's skills.' That took me by surprise. Was that coming from a man who loathed with passion the game I cherished all my life?

And having asked him why he banned me from playing, he said:

'Banning you from basketball is not your fault. It's a fear I have had since your mother died. She loved basketball. She loved it so much that it killed her on the court.' That moved me to tears and I quickly wiped it off my face.

It dawned on me that mom lost her life to the heart attack while playing in the WNBA. And I never knew it was a genetic disorder until the revelation now from dad.

'I figured if I let you play on the school court, you would get it out of your system. Now, I see I am wrong. So you can play!' He spilt it out and it falls on me like a rushing rain.

'I can?' The question rushed out of my mouth though I wasn't so sure where it came from. Dad's response was affirmative though he ordered I get a physical every six months which was non-negotiable.

'I guess I can wait until tomorrow to start your punishment. Go on and have fun with your team.' He beamed a once upon a time smile I used to know him with.

This was the best truth I could ever have heard in my lifetime from the one whom I cherished most. I hugged him so tight that I felt this is the best time I could best enjoy my life as a free born. Following his permission, I scurried off to the bus. I could feel he was watching me as he always does. That was how my passion was allowed to make headway after lots of perseverance.